the bull-jean stories

the bull-jean stories

by

sharon bridgforth

RedBone Press
Austin, TX

the bull-jean stories

Copyright © 1998 by sharon bridgforth

Published by:

RedBone Press
P.O. Box 1805
Austin, TX 78767

98 99 00 01 02   10 9 8 7 6 5 4 3 2 1

First edition

Cover illustration and design by Juarez Hawkins © 1998
Logo design by Mignon Goode
Printed in the United States of America

ISBN 0-9656659-1-7 $12.00

Dedication

for luz/my mina come stay   my daughter/my
beautiful flower   my mom/my guardian Angel
my son/my teacher   and my grandmother and
great-aunts who whisper from the other side.

Acknowledgements

some of these stories appear in (performance pieces): lovve/rituals & rage, no mo blues, dyke/warrior-prayers, blood pudding and passages of a bitta fruit.

much lovve and many thanks to the people who have encouraged, supported, witnessed, re-viewed, mentored, produced, presented, per-formed and nurtured my work   to my Angel friends who have tended my sanity, sobriety, and Spirit when I didn't have the sense or strength to   to lori d. wilson for helping me make the root wy'mn dream come to Life   and most especially to the one wo'mn of root wy'mn's one wo'mn shows/my Soul-sista sonja parks, who gave breath to the folk of these stories with her talent, creative vision and deep understanding of what i was trying to say. "poop monsta you is every wo'mn!"

big thanks to ms. redbone/ms. lisa moore. i am eternally grateful for the space, Faith, the gentle direction and commitment/the opportunity to be my Black lesbian-nonlinear writing self within the pages of a redbone press book. Life is good/yeah!

Preface

i am a child of the motown era/raised on aretha
franklin, bobby blue bland, bb king/grits, greens
and smothered porkchops. my mother migrated
west (the promised land) but carried her southern sensibilities with her: we listened to gospel
music on sundays (in lieu of church service);
revered the dead; and recognized music, food,
dancing, telling tales and laughing as a way to
heal/and pray.

in the tradition of my upbringing, **the bull-jean
stories** are performance stories/part of not
separate from Life and Ancestral Spirits. i see
the bull-jean stories as a blues quilt/each story
an individual composition that speaks on
survival and love/together creating a complete
picture of one wo'mn's journey through many
Life-times learning emotional and Spiritual
balance. bull-jean rarely speaks but when she
does/it is most often in the form of poetry
the language of the Heart.

with **the bull-jean stories** i wanted to celebrate
the rural/southern working-class Black
bulldaggas/who were aunty-momma-sister-
friend/pillars of the church   always been
a working part of our community/giving fierce
Love with fineness. the songs of my childhood/
the laughter/the gift of tale-telling/the food that
my elders gave me are integral parts of who i
am. though i can't dictate their particular words
i do understand that the voice of **the bull-jean
stories** belongs to them. these are the stories

they didn't tell me   the ones i needed most.
bull-jean is the butch/southern/poet/warrior
wo'mn hero i wish i'd known.

i hope you enjoy this dance/this taste of creat-
ing-remembering with me...

Table of Contents

Chapter 1

Chapter 2

Chapter One

bull-jean

&

sassy b. gonn

there go bull-jean and she aunty

      sassy b. gonn.

ever wednesday/twice on sundays

bull-jean go git she aunty   walk to the sto.

sassy old as dirt/cain't hear/don't memember

      today/done

drank she near-blind ass half to hell

and bull-jean

Lovve her/go git she aunty

ever wednesday

twice on sundays

walk to the sto.

sassy be talking loud enough to disturb the dead

say

1

lawd/baby

you walks lik yo

bloods is on you   all-blacker in the face/eyes

sunked/and

jes look at you

you been fuckn!

i done tole you/you cain't be fuckn ten days befo yo

bloods!

yessuh

ole sassy liable to say anythang.

secret is

to dress warm

cause if you gits a cold in yo cock/it'll go straight to

yo head   kill you fo time.

na/one wednesday sassy got sick clear through

sunday   in bed.

bull-jean had to call ole doc benson who was

breathing in sassy's face wid him eye-light when

she came to

lawd

that hefa cain't run no furtha than she can piss

but i declare she quick   reached

under that bed whipped up she shooter

had that man pent to the wall

fo he could take him next breath. sassy say

you touch me/i'll kill yo soul

and dare yo Spirit to rise

          she done had a flash-back

i'll tare yo Heart out

and spit-in-the-middle.

bull-jean in the back jesa hollering

3

aunt-momma/aunt-momma

give me the gun aunt-momma!

sassy say

since when you start coming cross the tracks.

you wouldn't come ova here when my baby came

twisted out the womb

you wouldn't come

when them hooded beasts burned the skin

offa my man/and

gottdamn   you didn't come when they snatched

my sister-split she limbs

taking turns on her back   i figa /you got enough

blood on yo hands from no-care

i ain't giving you nonna mines.

parently

sassy done forgot

she useta forgave the white peoples

you betta git on away from we!

well

ventually/bull-jean got the gun from she aunty.

na/sassy add that story to the other six she tell

ova

and ova

cept she don't memember being sick

some how

it all change to how she likta kill a man trying to

save bull-jean.

yessuh

they be walking

bull-jean and she aunty.

ever na and again

sassy look up   lik she seeing bull-jean fo the

first time-the-day

say

hey baby

when you join up?

sassy smile/take bull-jean's face

cup-in-both-hands

look the gurl in the eyes

say

you know/you always was

my favorite   we

cut from the same rug/we.

bull-jean smile/say

yes ma'am.

they walk on

hand-n-hand

stroll down the way

ever wednesday

twice on sundays

when bull-jean go git she aunty

sassy b. gonn   walk to the sto.

bull-jean

slipn in

ever day

5am

deacon willie/clara's man

go git him

supplies   umph

everbody know

nappy love

be the one filling him sack.

every day

5am

deacon willie/clara's man

slip out   bull-jean

slip in

      clara git her supplies too.

9

bull-jean say

one GOOD thirty minutes

lasts a Life-time

umph bull-jean and clara

got mo Life-times than a cat's times infinity   i know

cause i been watching them bout that long.

      not that i'm nosey or nuthn/cause

      i got business of my own you see/but

every day

5:30am

bull-jean slip out

look ruffled/smile dusty

eyes rolled   tongue damn near wagging

close yo mouth gurl i say

she don't hear

jes float on down the way.

one morning

5:30am

i jes snatch her on in sit down/talk right-in-her-face

bull-jean when you gonn smell the coffee

that gal is married! i said

blam/slam her some coffee so strong

it don't move in the cup.

bull-jean say

i been giving away tastes

piece by piece/samples

of my Heart/i

been giving for free   all my Life

it's almost gonn/my Heart

all i really want

is a kind word

and a smile

and that wo'mn is kind

and she Lovves me   and

it don't matter if it's thirty minutes a day

or ONCE in the next Life

11

i'll go git her/smile

whenever she'll let me

have it!

bull-jean go back to looking drifty.

umph/seem to me they be doing more than smiling

ova there.

then one day

5am

deacon willie/clara's man

didn't slip out

but bull-jean slippd in

shiit

i got my gun

figured all hell would break loose ova there

and spread my way

i waited

and

waited

5:05am

deacon willie/clara's man come out

tail dragging

sit on the porch holding him head

till 5:30am

bull-jean come out the FRONT door

and nodd him good-bye

struttn!

na/everbody know

the deacon was doing nappy love

but it turned out

deacon willie/clara's man

also been squeezing frosty jackson's onion

and frosty got mo sugga in him shorts

than the sto got sacks to hold it in

13

so i guess that make the deacon

semi-sweet.

bull-jean tole ole deacon

unless he want her to tell the wind/he better

go git some money from him honey

cause he was moving out

and she was moving in!

ain't no mo

slipn in/or out

ova there.

all i see is bull-jean and clara floating round

smiling.

ever na and then they come ova

sit wid me   looking drifty.

i give em some of my strong-ass-coffee

but they don't seem to smell it

and that makes me

smile.

bull-jean

&

that wo'mn

cleandra marie la beau

say she lik the way i

tickle her spot/say

folk keepa fiddling round but cain't seem to

find it/lik

 i can   she

take my hand   place it on her Heart/say

that's

my spot bull-jean/and since you touch it so sweet

i'm gonn let you see what else of mine

you can find to tickle...

oh/i'm so in Lovve   till

i'm sick/jes

hurt

17

all ova

body

   ache

mind

   sore

Heart

   hurt/jes

hurt

and it all began when i looked in the eyes of

THAT WO'MN.

na/i's a wo'mn

whats Lovved many wy'mns.

me/they call bull-dog-jean   i say

thats cause i works lik somekinda ole dog

trying to git a bone or two

they say it's cause i be sniffing after wy'mns

down-low/begging and thangs

whatever.

one day

i was sitting in my yard

telling tales and dranking wid my pal lou   when

i thought i heard a rustling

   i didn't look up cause the dogs was jes

   laying-round-not-saying-a-thang

   usually they barks at everythang

cluding me

so i jes kepa-dranking and telling

till i heard a voice

     hello

well i lik to fell ova in the petunias

sounded lik heaven to me

i looked round and lawdy-mercy

what i have to do that fo/na

i know you done heard this befo

19

but this wo'mn is here to testify:

DON'T MESS WID THEM FULL-GROWN

FULL-FLEDGE/SHO-NUFF-HOT-BUTT

WY'MNS!

they'll drop a spell on you quicker'n you can say

please

chile

i looked up and SHE caught me

wid her eyes   i ain't got loose yet.

fo the longest i didn't even see the rest of her

so lost in them eyes/deep

clear/flickering brown/Spirit-talking eyes

   take me na lawd   i said

   fo one moment in them eyes and i done lived

   full-in-yo glory

cain't recall much was said right away

too busy staring in them eyes.

fo the longest i didn't even see the rest of her

then i saw lips/full and quick to smile

   loose me lawd/git me out her spell

   i said   mouth watering/i thought

bet she sho know how to do some good Lovvn/lips so

fine and all.

fo the longest i didn't even see the rest of her

then i looked on down and saw nipples lunging/hips

ready to roll

sweet glory in the morning

   i'm done seen an angel

   in the form of flesh

thats when i gave up the ghost

jes said

here

fo i know'd SHE was the kinda wo'mn make you want

to give it up/say

baby

  take me

take all i got

take all i'll ever git

tell me

what you want gal

here

i'll give it jes to see you smile.

fate were standing before me

giving me a big brown hello.

and sho-nuff

i done spent all the rest of my days

tickling a permanent smile on that wo'mn's face.

bull-jean

&

trouble

i knew

trouble had done left   when i saw bull-jean sitting at

the b.y.o. wid jucey la bloom

i knew

trouble was gonn

cause jucey don't drank

and bull-jean don't hang

lessn some wo'mn done broke she Heart/and baby

bull-jean musta sho-nuff been hurting

cause jucey had done drank the fat part of a rat's ass

jigg'd.

you see bull-jean and jucey la bloom

friends from last-Life/they so close

they feel one-the-other's pain

jucey say

i think

i'll begin life again   come back

a dog/cock my leg or squat   bow-wow-mafucka

folk gonn haveta deal wid MY shit

next time round

yessuh/they business jes skooch-ova to my table

      cause you know i ain't a nosey-wo'mn.

jucey say

she ain't nuthn but a periodic-ho   ain't even got sense nuff

to charge on a regular basis.

bull-jean sit

holding she head

low to the table   stream-a-tears

rolling down the left side she face/her

don't bat a eye/nor make sound.

jucey on the other hand

jesa howling/rocking backwards and forwards/eyes

rolling

why/bull-jean/why you git we in this mess gurl

why?

bull-jean raise up

say

trouble/came in

stood to the side

  made me

    sense her first

russling skirt/jiggling jewelry/clicking

heels   trouble/came in

smelt lik sunshine   lik

freedom on a bed of posies/trouble

made me want her

befo i ever saw her face   she

entered my Heart

and held me/trouble

came in   ass popping

from side to side

she carried me across the room in her gaze/i

25

got lost

haven't found my way back

from trouble/she holds me

in her smile   i fit

between the moist on her lips/i

fit between her ears/i fit

in the middle of her intent/i fit

at the end of her fingers

i fit

in the pressure of her voice/her

heat as it lifts me/at the tip

of her thoughts as they extend themselves/wid

the extent of her desire/i

fit   i done laid down wid trouble/and

cain't

git

   up!

trouble came in

stood to the side

and took me

home.

jucey la bloom

jes hugged she head and she bottle

and cried.

bull-jean's

elements of lovve

you are Earth   i am Ocean

let me

cast my waters

up on

yo sho.

you are Sun

i is Moon/moving

to envelop

the distance

from out

our way.

you are Fire   i am Wind

oh/how i wants to

blow yo flame!

na see/that gurl

ain't got no sense.

be out under

sugga-sweet's

window   every

friday/come Moon-up

moaning

i will dance wid you through time

endure all thangs in yo embrace

smiling

as Life brings us closer

if this is not my destiny/then

i must Live again   because

nuthn

in this world

can keep me from you

   not even death...

umph/her gonn die alright

sugga gonn

ignore

the Life outta she.

cain't tell bull-jean that

though/she say

her and sugga Souls married last-Life/ain't

done yet

there are no words

fo some thangs   lik

the way my eyes

delight in yo's

lik

the sweetness of closen you   the

smell of yo breath in mine/yo

softness filling me/on you knowing

us full   there

are no words

fo some thangs

lik

the way you move me/yo

voice touching my Heart/lik

feeling

beyond-feeling/there

are

no words for

what you mean

to me/there

are

no

words   won't

you

let

me

make expression

for the thangs

language won't

let

me

say

  gal?

i sits out wid my cup

ever

friday/come Moon-up   listen to they

na/far as i can make-out

bull-jean ain't made-out yet.

sugga won't let her in the house/and

won't come out   jes

lean from the window a spell

then shut the shade

shiit

some nights

all bull-jean

can get out is a croon'n

lawd/lawd/lawd

oh my

lawd/lawd/lawd

oh lawd

it take bugga to tell it though

bugga is sugga's gran-aunty on she daddy's side who be

my aunt butta's ex-husband/uncle chain's

second-wife's sista

anyway

bugga-sweet

counsel wid bull-jean

say

na/i

done had

34

enough

pussaay

to last till i returns

you

on the other hand

needs

some gurl

i don't know

what

you done-done

to that gal last-Life

but i don't reckon she near-fixnta

let you Lovve her this one

so go on wid yo-self!

na/first off

look lik bugga ain't had enougha nuthn

cause i seen nuckie-little

crawling out she window

jes last week

looking lik that ole no-tooth-hefa done ju-ju she draws

course i got better thangs to do than watch the goings on

at the sweet house

 i jes cain't stand to see po bull-jean suffering so

   i done tried to git her to come

   ova here fo tea

   steada ova there

   fo misery

anyway

bugga say

go on

git you one them

seasoned-suzzies/a

big-bettye or a

tight-tammye.

you needs

a ready ripe-wrapped/done-done-it

wo'mn.

and if you feels

anythang

what resemble Lovve

RUN!!!

cause you know

you cain't handle it/be

ova here all looped up

and thangs.

bull-jean

let that nine-Life cat

jesa-keepa-talking

till nuckie-little come by

whistle bugga to the bushes.

bull-jean sit there

looking

con-fused

till

up come the shade

and out the window

stick sugga she head

bull-jean say

sugga

all i want to do

is give yo thoughts affection

soothe yo feelings wid kindness

and give yo dreams some Lovvn.

i won't be trying to touch

nuthn but friendship

if thats all you want

to give me.

chile

the shade

neva went down

that night.

next thang i know

bull-jean

IN THE HOUSE WID SUGGA

friday/come Moon-up/stay till Moon-down.

all i hear is laughter/the

smell of

chicken

sizzln

39

and

the sound of bugga running

through the bushes

cause she cain't break loose the spell

she put on nuckie-little!

bull-jean

&

next-Life/blues

this is the story of

Lovve ain't enough

it's about

fear and saddness/and

next-Life

blues

this

is the story of

one wo'mn's

struggle to ungrip

she Soul

from misery...

41

na/it all

began

befo i know   and it all

ended

full-Moon day/some time

ago/middla

safirra louise goode's

wedding.

safirra   the reverend peter goode sr.'s

only

gurl/sweet

as she is

rotten.

got a slow grin/a

ripe ass

and enough

of the devil in her

to drive any good fool

madd.

her   promised to

sampson tucka johnson/the reverend

e.m. johnson's

youngest/owner of

tucka's joint

cross the county line.

the two reverends figa

between they

two sinning off-spring

at least one God fearing child

oughts to be got.

safirra figa she

make her daddy happy

and

43

enjoy tucka's fast life and long money/tucka

figa he get

some good help

and free lovvn.

so it was on

the biggest

two-preacha-four-choir-twelve-deacon

high rolling broom-jump

of all time.

only thang

bout it

safirra   bull-jean's wo'mn!

hell

everbody

know it

safirra

ain't nuthn but two-sided/walk

ever whicha way/lik she gots to have it all   mens

in the street/bull-jean

in the sheets/jes

all-of-it

po bull-jean.

spoil that wo'mn/jes lik the gurl daddy   let she have

her way

all the time

but ever body know

safirra

done gonn too far

this time

tole bull-jean

baby/if you Lovves me

lik you say you do

you gots to want to

share in this most important

event in my life

say

after all

my Heart

belongs to

you /you

the one

i really

Lovves/always

will find a way

to get to you

momma.

umph

chile

folk was all up in that church house

come broom-jump time/jes

packed   fanning and showing out

waiting and all/they was up in there/um-hmm

anyway

everthang

was jes-beautiful

till the reverend e.m. ask

do anyone here

have cause to object

to this matrimonial binding

of god's choosing?

bull-jean

stood

up

had on she best suit/pressed and all

say

looka here

this

ain't no binding/and it

sho ain't none of God's choosing   i

the one put on this earth

to walk wid that wo'mn and/i

the one oughta be up there wid her na/so

yessuh

mr. reverend preacha man

i take the right

to make objection

to this

lie-befo God.

SAFIRRA

you my

biscuits and gravy

the amen

at the end of my prayers   you

my perfumed hallelujah

            sweet chariot stop and let me ride/you

my southern comfort

my gi-tar

stroking

all night

cradling the scent of you/are

my memories/you are

all the wy'mn i have

ever

Lovved   my

last-Life-Lovve

come back/my

new Moon

dancing across a cool stream

you

are settled

in the depths of me

and no matter where you go

who you wid

or what you do

you

is

MINES!!!

chile

you coulda heard

a mouse fart.

cept ole

conchita la fraud

and she sista weewee

had they black asses

giggling in the back of the church/slurping and

fussing ova they sack drank

   at po bull-jean's most serious moment

anyway

bull-jean

jes stand there

say

saddness/settle in the bones

you know   it rots

the will and puts out

the fires of Life.

you gonn be sad

wo'mn

cause i'm fixnta

be gonn

and i ain't

gonn be dead.

bull-jean

look safirra

in the eye/real hard

say

i may not

be able to promise

you fancy rangs

and furs and thangs

but i guarantee

that when we kiss

you'll hear the Angels sang   and

if that ain't enough

to fill yo Life wid joy

and comfort

i

release

you

na

Lovve.

her turn and walk out.

safirra pass out

boom!

all up in the sanctuary

lik some body done snipped she cord-a-Life.

ain't

been the same since

done gained twenty pounds

each side the hip   butt drop

eyes dull/even

the devil done left her   she

sanctified na

jump and holla

everwhere

cept in bed   i hear she

neva do help tucka neitha

anyway

bull-jean

she bitta.

sit round

sangn the same

sorryass thang all the time

Lovve

will kill you

break yo Heart

in two

say/Lovve

will kill you

break yo Heart

in two

i'm so

sick of Lovve

i don't know

what to do.

i done tried to tole her

see/yo mind and yo mouth

left the wo'mn   but

yo soul

still gripped round that ass/clangn

on fo dear life

you best pry it free

fo you be stuck wid that gurl fo all time.

her no hear me/naw

too busy wading in bittaness

Lovve

will kill you

break yo Heart

in two

i'm so

sick of Lovve

i don't know

what to do.

bull-jean

&

the power of no mo

there is so much

silence

widout you.

it's the hardest thang   i'll

never get used to/this

silence widout you

i

am trapped

by my own space/my

memory remains locked

in your voice   forcing

me to grieve the days

of our discontent.

silence holds me na

and keeps me

restless

in the absence

of you.

useta be

sweet

thoughtful minded

  helpful handed

    empathy actioned   useta

wouldn't mind/give

my last smile

to my wo'mn-useta all

talk about how sweet i be

well

i

ain't sweet

no mo   put sweet out

myself

sweet

ain't got me

nuthn

but left.

i done decided

no mo

no mo

sleeping wid sorrow in

a empty bed   no mo

longing what cain't

be filled/no mo

yo-last-visit-ghost give

me haint'd Heart/cain't

get drunk enough mind scarred   i

ain't chasing the blues

no mo.

it's time

i

settle down

wid me!

Chapter Two

bull-jean

is b.j. la rue

i na know   the secret of

b.j. la rue.

b.j.

live what you call a

sportn life   sports

different wy'mns/all the time

      till ole mary boutté come long/neva-left.

b.j.

sang somewhere uptown

leave round dinner

come back at lunch   tuesday

thru sunday

      till ole mary boutté come long.

b.j.

pressed/always

crisp   wear black

short sleeve shirt show

how hard the meat packed/bagged

pants belted up

winged out-fresh shined shoes

skin

greased

hair

low

  slick

   b.j. be sportn

i been trying to find out

where that club is

       so i can go/get me some   sangn-to

anyway

somethang bout b.j. have always twitched my mind

couldn't figure zackly what it were

then it come to me

b.j. la rue   BULL-DOG-JEAN

yessuh!

see

back home

my momma's sista live next to the dutrey house

by the crawfish hole ova to the la rue's.

the la rue boys

hittn-stick/strang-finga/song/and horn-head

is musical

hittn-stick boy tootie/marry ms. nu-moon gurl/had

too many babies/sent the oldest to

they city sista   i thankn

i ain't neva seen the child

till i heard b.j. sangn

i'd lik to be

the coffee in yo cup

the first thang

you put your lips on

65

each day

i'd lik to be

the coffee in yo cup

what you grind

at night

to get on your way

her trying to get ole mary boutté

to let her back in the house

sound jes lik she daddy tootie/ms. nu-moon gurl man

i said

baby/you ain't got to stand in that yard/sangn fo suppa/i gots

plentya food right

here

anyway

parently the club owners twist off she name

make more money letting the mens think

her a man-sangn-man-sorrows

tell you what

them wy'mn's know her a she

be all flocked round

i hearing she don't even hardly try to make no

business wid em

jes hug up/talk/have tea   listen to they

then ole mary boutté come long

tore that playhouse down!

i said/jes tell me why you had to invite mary stay.

bull-jean say

it was the way she smiled at me/wid her eyes

pouty lips/parted

deep breath laugh/the

Sun resting on her neck

head back

a little to the side   it was

67

the way one strap

fell slightly off her shoulder

breasts sitting playful

waist

curvn/hips

turned in seat

jes a bit.

it was the way she knew me

wid her smile

that told me

this wo'mn was home.

umph.

anyway

bull-jean

still sporty-dress in black-packaged hard/cept na

go uptown/after dinner

be home by dusk   tuesday thru saturday

ole mary make she go to church

ha!

    let me

    be the coffee in yo cup

    hold me close/smell

    your memories

    wake

    black/wid

    a little sugar

    made to fit your taste

    stir and sip me slow

    don't let none go to waste

    i need to be yo coffee baby

    long as you want your cup filled up/i'd

    lik to be the coffee/baby

    waiting for you   in yo cup.

bull-jean

got read

they got read   not red lik the colour but read lik

she can read music therefo she well

read

um hmm

they got read/bull-jean gonn get her na.

read overto the jailhouse hollern

i'ma good mafuckn citizen/why you got me chaindup

lik this   mafuckas

if read name wasn't read it'd be mafucka cause she

mafucks us to death round here.

her niece babygurl gets it the most though/when every

sunday after church babygurl holds reads licka hostage

read chase babygurl down the street

give me my mafuckn bottle

back

mafucka

i don't know why read bother run

gonn get a bottle by friday/when

she sang her drunk ass round town fo dranks.

bull-jean useta run wid read   hard

but since babett left

bull-jean don't drank no mo/don't run none

babett

  babett johnson/not babett dushard/the dushards is

  my relation/the johnsons belong to tufus and them-on

  they daddy's aunty's husband side/which is why i

  know all this cause my cousin pooky

  married tufus uncle brother

um hmm.

bull-jean still trying to get babett back

talk to me

tell me

what you want

i'd lik to know/whats

on your mind   whats

going on inside you/baby

talk to me

please

respond...

um hmm

bull-jean and read usta start friday hit the road/hit every

club crossing three county lines   by sunday morning

be back at the country mile propped

for the late last show.

make babett stay home wait/while she badd ass ack-out

all ova everwhere.

but since babett left

73

bull-jean walk away from her bottle and her bad ackn

my Heart hurts

from reaching

for you/you're not here

i need to

see your smile

smell you/have your laughter

dear   i am so lonely

say you'll see me

just once more

i thirst for you.

quench me quick/give me

your skin/touch me

let me turn to you

and sleep.

baby/babett done broke that wo'mn down.

see/babett from what you calls

a musical family

the daddy's-daddy pass it   they all play

some form of instrument

some in a classical way some/honky-tonk but they all

plays

thats how babett met bull-jean/cause read

was taking lessons from babett daddy

bull-jean tag along cause practice on friday right befo

getround time.

well

Lovve is nice and all

but babett wasn't no messround gurl

had thangs to do songs to play

couldn't do nuthn wid all the mess bull-jean kept round.

i always hoped to hold you

to treasure you/i meant to

be kind

75

and thoughtful and clear   i wanted to

never leave

never take you for granted/to honor

each moment

i intended

to love you well.

shiit   babett gonn/and

thankyoujesus heavenly saints angels and holy ancestors

bull-jean don't drink no mo!

read

on the other hand done loss her family/fine clothes/

pocket change   and her front teef   still dranking

bull-jean gonn get her na

neva get babett back though/cause

sometimes you cain't get back what a ass done loss

following a sick mind

um hmm/yeah.

bull-jean

at big briggette's

the room was full   we

carried disappointment heavily/though

loudly we laughed the world out our heads/for

jes a moment

we found ease/being Coloured

in america/it was our day of rest

late friday till mid-sunday

at club seeyaround   late

friday till mid-sunday

bull-jean was there.

at her table in the corner in the front

  she waited

    lik everbody else

        cept bull-jean wasn't gripped on a drank

        lik some of us/no

cause drank

done already made her dead

and crazy/well but

thats a whole nutha story/yeah.

then it happened

serafine agata santiago showed herself on stage

her don't jes walk out

she appear

wavy black-brown/thick hipped/curvy tasty/fiiine

chocolate

a collection of rhythms/kept-sounds

body released variations of layers of

syncopated memories from

many times back

feet-da dadada da hips-swish swish dip and swirl head-turn

and stare and turn/stare and turn fingers-snappn clap clap

snap snappn pouch poutn lips smile

smile

all light ray-out in one blink.

her don't jes walk out/she vision forth

and when she unleash that voice

all hell break loose/yeah   the peoples

jes lose they mind

　　　i grab my zin-zin and pray

　　　cause i know her done worked up a juju

　　　long befo

　　　she open her mouth/sang

　　　well but thats a whole nutha story/yeah

　　　　meet me when the leaves change

　　　　meet me when the boatbell clang

　　　say/meet me when the leaves change

　　　　meet me when the boatbell clang

79

i'ma take you down the river

gonn make you holla/make you sang

say/meet me baby

jes want you to come half-way

say/meet me baby

gonn show you what words cain't neva say

na/only fools

and strangers

even thank bout ackn-out in club seeyaround

cause

the proprietress   big briggette

will not only kick yo ass/she will

hunt you down-tare yo home to the ground

then tell yo mamma.

you ask for it/if you ack-out in

big briggette's place/yeah

80

it is said she can suck all the air out the room/use it

to knock the head off yo body   in one blow

    well but you know

    thats a whole nutha story/yeah!

na/we all know

everbody ack-a-fool

sometime

baby

it musta been fool's nite out at club seeyaround that

nite/cause

wasn't a stranger in site.

    na/historical fact is

    we done most often fought onetheother because

    somebody's somebody thought they somebody

    done done it wid somebody else/yeah

well

serafine sangn

somethangs gota hold of me

i cain't let go

somethangs gota hold of me

the only thang i know

is i want to do what we said

we wasn't gonn do no mo

say/i want to do what we did

lik we done it befo

lil red lilly musta thought her tufus thought serafine

was sangn to her/yeah/cause

bam   lilly knock ole tufus upside her head right there

front center table

papa ann got up out her seat from back the room

thats when i knew some shit was fixn to happen

everbody but tufus know lil red lilly is papa ann's

midnight delight

don't lik to see lil lilly upset   came up

front center table

broke a bottle of some good licka on tufus head

big briggette stood up

everbody stopped breathing/jes

stopped

see/big briggette don't walk/no

she re-arrange the room getting from place to place

her reach ova toss ole tufus clear out the club

then step out after she

tufus mamma was there went on out too/madd cause

tufus done pause our good-got-damn-day of rest

see/some time a fool jes sitting round

being theyselves is enough to cause trouble.

well/we all get back to breathing

serafine

start up again/sangn beaming right into bull-jean's

eyes/putting a work on bull-jeans grinning ass foreal

well but thats a whole nutha story/yeah.

bull-jean & mina

stay

i from da swamp. my fo-matha

snap two man neck/run free ta swamp people/we

long time from here

da ship ova stop at island

trade fo-matha man

fo wata   fo-fatha kill/oh six   seven

fin freedom too.

since dat time we people go from island ta swamp

be wid one da otha

dats how mina git here/she island gurl sent

by my uncle elias firs born daughta chile/when she

small small

she not my baybay   but is.

on dis day   mina sit

mumble mumble/suck teef   her madd at bull-jean.

bull-jean sit/sit no talk   stuck

done let so many wrong-words out cain't fin

da right ones no mo.

i been tole bull-jean *git on-way gurrl*

come back when you got some right words.

bull-jean tuck'd tail leave come back leave come back

go ta she gran-granny's/tryn think

find some right words fo mina

still on dis day sit sit no talk/words stuck in mouth.

so useta havn she way bull-jean is

all da time all da wy'mns give her everthang

cept stay   bull-jean use dat as cause ta

ack-out no git long no work it out   no stay.

i telln her

problem is

you been barkn at da wrong tree   if you know

you lookn at a cat

why you spect it ack lik a dog

a cat-is a cat/ain't nuthn but

a cat   why you mad cause it ain't a dog/you da dog

gurrl!

bull-jean want mina stay mus talk no-bark no act-out

cause mina see a barkn dog/move on

bull-jean cain't capture mina/mina got ta want come

stay.

mina say

> *why you trying to call me yo wife bull-jean*
>
> *wife*
>
> *what do that mean anyway?*
>
> *i been called wife befo*
>
> *turned my whole Life ova to the concept/to*
>
> *obey to have foever till death   i done*
>
> *that/already died once*
>
> *wasting prayers on makebelieve/rose*
>
> *up from a bed of lies/untended*

wilted and left   woke up robbed

of precious time and sweet joy

look lik   wife

is a word folk use when they want

license to control you   if you trying

to claim me bull-jean/jes call me yo wo'mn

that's what i am

a wo'mn

complete

wid or widout you   i'll be

yours/long as its right

but i need you to tell me

what you want/exactly what

you asking me   cause

wife

ain't saying nuthn right/in my mind!

umph/dey go bak ta it

bull-jean standn/wid a badd case of da tongue tied

mina sitn   wid da sour con cepts

mumble mumble suck teef

        i jes tryn ta blend wid da wood

        cain't go in da houze not know

sit sit mumble stand

silent

silent/blend

umph

dey givn me da tight heart

den looka

bull-jean come foward   on knees ta mina

hold hands/take eyes say

        mina tisono

        i bull-dog-jean

        am asking you to be my wo'mn

        whole and complete   in all essence

        i want to make this journey/this Life

89

wid you   i want to wake

to the smell of your hair/the taste

of your neck   each morning/i

want you curled into me so i can

turn you open/to the

light of your eyes

i want to offer all the tenderness

and consideration i am capable

of /and more   gently/i want

to treasure tomorrows possibilities

wid you

exchange dreams/walk through the challenges

of the day/share minds wid you

mina i want to Pray   in the

curve of your hips the turn of your

lips the wet of your kiss/i want

to praise God for the Blessing of you.

as long as it's right

i want you to

stay

be who you are wid fierceness

be honest wid me

and see me when you look

that is what i want/that's

what i am asking   be

my wo'mn mina

bull-jean breathe those last words into mina

be my wo'mn mina

three times

and three times mina breathe back

i'm yo wo'mn bull-jean

be mine

yeah/i go in da houze na wid a

strong Heart knowin da future

done finally laid down wid Lovve...

bull-jean's aunt tilly

na/i shoots mafuckas.

yessuh   run through

my yard   crawlout.

shiitt

buttfullalead be fair warning to where my next aim

jes might be...

thats tillecous loufina johnson

the reverend e.m. johnson's mother's oldest

 sista-moved to the city sometime ago/to seek she

fortune. we calls her ole tilly fo short.

she did acquire a fortune

        just don't nobody know how

anyway

most days bout all ole tilly do is sit on her porch

till saturday night/getta shooting at them

near-grown children what run through she yard.

na/ole tilly can shoot a can off a squirrel's ass blindfold

so i know   she don't really

want to hit them half-grown fools

just lik to cuss up on the threat

hell she help raise they mammas and daddys

which is why each one speaks when they pass

>   *hey aunt tilly*

>   *how you today*

till saturday night they gets to shortcutn from trouble

straight into ole tilly's barrel

hollering fallnout running and carrying on

>   saturday nights/most folk jes sit out

>   wait for the fools to show up-ackout

>   entertain we

till bull-jean come stay wid ole tilly.

see/bull-jean's great aunty

puddn

live wid ole tilly near fifty years

till puddn pass from sugga/too high pressure

and a badd cough.

      that puddn was somefine   6ft. 300lbs. of bitta

        sweet carmel/yeah!

      puddn was the onlyess one ever could handle

        ole tilly

anyway

they sent bull-jean to see after she aunt tilly cause

word gotdown that the ole gal had been driving

on all sides the road

na/that hefa may could shoot blindfold

but she couldn't drive worth shit

especially after the sight situation settle on she.

first two months of bull-jean's stay ole tilly forgot bout

the chil'rens/took to cussn and shooting at bull-jean

who had hid the car keys   and the car.

well/finally ole tilly tireout

got back to she usual ackn-outs.

till one saturday night

me and bull-jean was on my porch conversatn/wid

cobbla and coffee

when we realize ain't been no noise long time after

fools time out.

well

bull-jean lightup outta there quick to she aunty's

found ole tilly sitting just as quiet

the kinda–grown chil'ren at her feet looking so sad

bull-jean scream

aunt t aunt t

what's wrong?

ole tilly look up say

nuthn baby   puddn come for me/that's all

told me i'd better say my good-byes.

but don't you worry none

i'll be back round/check on ya'll from time to time.

at that sudda's baby's gurl start to crying

 don't leave aunty/don't you leave us na

oh on and on.

well

it wasn't long after that.

ole tilly pass.

left the car the house and everthang of her and puddn's

to bull-jean.

bull-jean drove the car back to the country/to mina

let eura's gurl's boy and him wife-just-had-chile

have the house.

they name that baby loufina jr.

say ole tilly come by the baby's room

wid rumbling

na and again/carrying on in the early morning. say they

run in and jr. be just laughing and smiling lik she

playing wid she

best friend-visiting

well

but/that's a whole nutha story/yeah...

bull-jean

& the question of family

mamma mamma mamma mamma mamma mamma mamma

mamma mamma mamma mamm mamma mamma mamma

shiit

i cain't hardly step off my porch widout they noise

following me

mamma mamma mamma mamma mamma mamma mamma

mamma mamma mamma mamma mamma maaaaaaaammma

gotdamniit! what could they want so loud

ohh/my nerves is badd...

my name is pontificuss devine johnson

they calls me cuss for short. i lives by

mina and bull-jean and them chil'rens what be filling

they yard up. some is theys/some is nieces nephews

99

neighbors and cousins

shiit they all looks alik to me

noisy

mina send the chil'rens to make groceries for me friday

evenings   saturday mornings i goes to mina

help supervise the chil'rens yard work.

it was a saturday morning/i was sitting

supervising

lula mae's youngest daughter child/lil bitta

had just drop she son stank by

who was distracting me from my duties

 cause he jes kepa sticking his lil snot fingers in bull-

jean's ears climbing crawling playing her nose/wid

him toes   till he tire out went nap

under the peach tree

curled up next to mina's dog dooky

who head is big as my ass   and i gots plenty ass baby

        gotdamniit my ass is legendary in these parts!

buterra

mina sit wid me   supervise too/send bull-jean in the

house wid a list of thangs to work on. i figure i see

bull-jean next saturday many to-do's was on that sheet.

well i dose off

      let mina supervise on she own fo a time

till i feel dooky's tail beating the side of my chair

i open my eyes

and there standing this man   tall

tall/sapphire smooth/panther sleek

handsome as a newly crowned king.

i knew i knew him/but couldn't recall where from.

thought he was utility jones boy's child they sent off for

education/and a chance

cept that boy ain't step foot-called-nor writ back home

since he got him lawyerhood.

     heard he married white

     shiit we would have welcomed her too. he just

     so busy trying to forget who

he is he done forgot where he come from.

buterra

a closer look at the porch fella show a scar from eye to

chin down the right side his face.   muscles as big as

bull-jean's/hands knicked and callused

     make him not seem to be no desk man

     though he was sharp as a tack.

i see/mina know him right off/she jump up

hug him tight

then hold him scar in her hand and cry

call bull-jean out.

soon as bull-jean step to the porch/eye catch that man's

her had to sit down

     she Heart stop   i know cause i felt the pause

he go to her   sit at feet say

mamma.

i have missed you.

not a day has passed that i have not thought about you and

wanted to come home. after they first took me from you i cried

until there weren't no tears left in my twelve year old body.

i cried my Soul away/till my own tears flooded my Heart

gonn.

seemed lik nobody even saw me. they just took they bible

used it to beat down my Heart.

they called you unholy

a sinner gonn burn in hell   said you was unnatural

and unsafe for children to be around/that they'd see you

rot under the jail if i so much as stepped to your gate.

afterwhile i just got mad   at you.

you was the strongest smartest person i knew

yet you didn't have the power to carry me back home.

i hated you for that

for leaving me alone

and scared.

103

i ran off all the time/but they always had me found.

soon as i got near old enough i joined the service.

i wanted to fight/to die really.

i took the most dangerous jobs/the heaviest loads

the longest hours

saw the most shores

but everywhere i went everthang i did-there i was   so

misery went along for the ride.

somehow out of that small place i operated from/there must

have been room for light.

i know you was praying for me

i felt you   though i wouldn't let my mind tell me so.

you always was my Angel/my very own Saint.

it was you that taught me how to pray

how to tie my shoes/starch my pants/fish/fry

chicken/fight/play ball   you

taught me how to cut a rose and fix it nice for the table/how to have manners and talk to folk direct/and in the eye

i remember

you'd come home strained wid sweat/hands cut and cracking

legs dragged   but you always had a smile for me/always

a hug and

as much time as i needed.

really in them first twelve years of my life

you taught me how to be man.

but they took me from you and they didn't know nuthn about

smiling/storytelling

sangn me to sleep

or how to make a home safe for sweet dreams.

the man i became ain't the man you raised.

i have been selfish closed and driven by anger.

i been grievn mamma

all this time i been lost/unable find my way home

to feel my own Heart.

i didn't want to bring no children into that cruel world.

didn't have enough feelings

to keep a wo'mn   so i just kept going around the world

working wid a twisted mind.

then

one day i saw this little boy

 he was huddled up next to a dumpster

near night time

looking dirty and shivering. he looked up

caught my eyes

and there/i saw myself   full of pain fear and hopelessness.

i knew wasn't nuthn i could do but pray for him/for myself

to find God and hold on till the way home came clear.

i know i always knew how to get home

guess it wasn't time befo.

but today God is wid me

and i am carrying my Heart on my sleeve

proud and sure of the man i am

becoming again.

that boy/he didn't have no people   they was killed

in a tenement fire

so i adopted him. we taking good care of each other.

he's in the yard there

pulling that wagon me and you made long time ago.

i have missed you mamma.

but i'm back home na

and ain't nobody gonn come take us apart again

not in this Life!

gotdamniit

they had me crying so that day

i ain't been the same since.

bull-jean

she couldn't talk for a long time/just sit

hold the hands of her manchild/crying

out the left side she face

smiling.

bull-jean's son-man say he gots two mammas na/mo

Lovve-mo hugs-mo good cooking

mo joy fo him and the boy   they got a nice lil house

ova by the mammas. son-man do building work

teach the chil'rens building on friday nights.

        na/them sapsuckas gots another yard to run

        around screaming in

and gotdamniit

i think thats Blessed assurance that God is good/make

everthang alright in time

yeah!

ORDER FORM

To order single copies, send a check or money order for
$12.00 per book plus $3 shipping to:

RedBone Press
P.O. Box 1805
Austin, TX 78767

Name:

Address:

City: State:
Zip:

Telephone: (   )

DISTRIBUTED TO THE BOOK TRADE BY:

LPC Group
1436 West Randolph St.
Chicago, IL 60607
(800) 626-4330

ORDER FORM

To order single copies, send a check or money order for $12.00 per book plus $3 shipping to:

RedBone Press
P.O. Box 1805
Austin, TX 78767

Name:

Address:

City: State:
Zip:

Telephone: (   )

DISTRIBUTED TO THE BOOK TRADE BY:

LPC Group
1436 West Randolph St.
Chicago, IL 60607
(800) 626-4330